Zero
Grandparents

MICHELLE EDWARDS

Harcourt, Inc.

San Diego   New York   London

www.harcourt.com

Library of Congress Cataloging-in-Publication Data
Edwards, Michelle.
Zero grandparents/Michelle Edwards.
p.   cm.
"A Jackson friends book."
Summary: Calliope does not have a grandmother or grandfather
to bring to school on Grandparents Day, but she finds a special
way to participate anyway.
[1. Grandparents—Fiction.   2. Grandmothers—Fiction.
3. Schools—Fiction.]   I. Title.
PZ7.E262Ze 2001
[Fic]—dc21   98-11696
ISBN 0-15-202083-7

C E G H F D
Printed in Hong Kong

The illustrations in this book were done in pen and ink,
ink wash, and white paint on Arches hot press watercolor paper.
The display type was set in Worcester Round Medium.
The text type was set in Sabon.
Manufactured by South China Printing Company, Ltd., China
This book was printed on Arctic matte paper.
Production supervision by Sandra Grebenar and Pascha Gerlinger
Designed by Lydia D'moch and Michelle Edwards

To Meera, Flory, and Lelia,
who would have been terrific grandchildren

To the memory of Lil and Sis,
who would have been terrific grandmas

And to all kids with zero grandparents…

This book is for you.

Contents

Howardina Geraldina Paulina Maxina Gardenia Smith

Calliope Turnipseed James

Pa Lia Vang

The Big News

Calliope James raced to school. Second grade at Jackson Magnet was great.

Calliope and her two best friends, Howie and Pa Lia, were all in the same class. Mrs. Fennessey's class. Room 201. Calliope sat behind Pa Lia. Howie sat behind Calliope. Three best friends, all in a row.

Calliope said hi to her best friends. She gave each of them a super smile and slid into her seat. She took out her pencil and checked the point. *Not sharp enough*, she thought.

GRIND, GRIND.

Calliope liked her pencil point very sharp.

GRIND.

Now she was ready.

Calliope could hardly wait for Mrs. Fennessey to say, "Time for math." Math was first thing every morning. Calliope loved math.

"Good morning, class," said Mrs. Fennessey.

Calliope sat up straight. She touched her pencil point.

Perfect.

"Before we start math today," said Mrs. Fennessey, "I have a very important announcement."

What could be more important than math? Calliope hoped they weren't going to do an art project. She hated getting glue all over her fingers.

"When everyone is quiet," said Mrs. Fennessey, "I'll know you are ready to hear the big news."

Maybe they were going on a field trip to the zoo, or to the children's museum or the planetarium. Calliope could feel her heart beating faster.

Field trips are the best, Calliope thought. She quickly folded her hands and waited.

A Special Day

"Next Wednesday will be Grandparents Day at Jackson Magnet," Mrs. Fennessey told the class. "You may bring your grandparents to school. We will have a welcome time and you can tell us all about them."

Calliope scrunched down in her seat.

"We will have a big party," said Mrs. Fennessey. "It will be a very special day."

Calliope felt the empty space between her two front teeth. She wrote zeros all over her notebook.

Zero. Zero. Zero.

Calliope had zero grandparents to bring to school. She had zero grandparents to welcome. They were all dead.

"Now, some of you might not have a grandparent to bring," said Mrs. Fennessey softly. "You may want to bring a special friend, or you may want to share a friend's grandparent."

Pa Lia turned around. She smiled at Calliope.

Howie tapped her on the shoulder.

Pa Lia and Howie had grandparents to share. They both had grandmas who lived with them.

Calliope scratched her arm. Her skin felt prickly and itchy. Her eyes felt warm and watery. She didn't want to share grandparents with her best friends.

Calliope wanted her own.

Zero Grandmas

Calliope burst into the kitchen. She threw her backpack down.

Slam.

"Is something wrong?" asked Mrs. James.

"Yes," said Calliope. She grabbed an apple and her big bag of Halloween candy. "Next Wednesday is Grandparents Day."

Calliope dumped all her candy on the table. "And I don't have any grandparents to bring." She took a big, loud bite of apple. *Chomp.*

"It isn't fair that all my grandparents are dead," said Calliope.

"I could come on Grandparents Day," offered Mrs. James.

"But you're not my grandmother," Calliope told her.

14

"With all this gray hair, who would know the difference?" her mother asked.

I would, thought Calliope. *And so would everyone else.*

"No thanks," said Calliope. She passed her mother a lollipop. Lollipops were Mrs. James's favorite.

If my grandma was alive, I'd share my Halloween candy with her, too. Calliope put four baby-sized chocolate bars next to her apple.

She counted her candy as she put it back in the bag. "…ninety-seven, ninety-eight, ninety-nine, one hundred."

Calliope James had one hundred pieces of Halloween candy and zero grandmas.

Grandma Goldie

Today the kids in room 201 were making paper crowns for Grandparents Day.

Yuck.

Calliope had to work with stinky Matthew Stern, the enemy of the second grade.

Double yuck.

"Time to clean up," announced Mrs. Fennessey. "Then we will have a story before lunch."

Calliope loved it when Mrs. Fennessey read aloud. She zipped over to the sink and washed the glue off her hands. She gathered scraps of paper from the floor and tossed them in the trash. When the room was clean, Mrs. Fennessey began.

"Today's story is about Grandma Goldie, a very special grandma," Mrs. Fennessey told the class.

Who wants to hear a dumb story about a grandma? Calliope wanted to plug her ears.

But Grandma Goldie *was* a special grandma. People said she could talk to animals. She was good and kind and wise. Her singing made plants and flowers grow big and tall. Her hugs could mend the most broken heart.

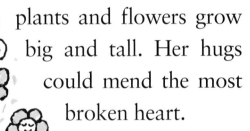

Calliope wished she had a Grandma Goldie to hug. *Why does everyone else have a grandma but me?*

"Wasn't that a great story?" Howie

said at lunch. "I just love that Grand-ma Goldie."

"*Brr.*" Calliope shivered. She felt cold. Her fingers were icy.

"What's wrong?" asked Pa Lia.

"Nothing, zero, zilch, nothing," Calliope answered.

"Have a cookie," said Howie. "One of Grandma Gardenia's Peanut Butter Delights."

Calliope took a cookie. *If my grand-ma was alive, we would bake cookies together every day.*

Calliope threw her lunch away.

"I hate Grandparents Day," she muttered.

Poor Calliope!
Where are Calliope's grandparents?
Doesn't Calliope have any grandparents?
Ha, Ha, Ha
Too Bad!
How sad!
Doesn't Calliope have anyone who loves her?
She should bring her dog.
I don't know wh
I'd do without my grandma.
Poor Calliope!
I'm glad my grandparents are alive.
Poor Calliope
Ha, H
Ha.
Don't you just feel sorry for Calliope?
If I were Calliope, and I didn't have even one grandma to bring, I'd stay home.
How sad!
Poor Calliope!
Poor Calliope!
How sa

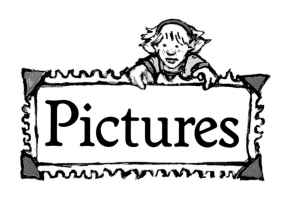

Pictures

Tomorrow the grandparents would come to school.

Calliope would be alone without a grandparent. Even Stinky Stern had a grandpa to bring.

Ha Ha! No Grandparents

Calliope's mother and father had offered to come. But they were not her grandparents.

Calliope sat on her bed and looked at pictures. Her father had given her a big album filled with them. There were pictures of her mother and father, her

aunts and uncles, and all of her cousins. In the very back, there was an old picture of her grandma Flory Sophia Turnipseed. She had died before Calliope was born.

Calliope took the picture of Flory Sophia and put it by her mirror.

She looked at Flory Sophia's warm smile. Calliope had a space between her two front teeth, just like Flory Sophia.

Flory Sophia June 1967

She looked at Flory Sophia's kind face. Calliope had freckles all over her face, just like Flory Sophia.

She looked at Flory Sophia's big hands. Calliope had big hands, just like Flory Sophia.

Calliope wished that Flory Sophia weren't dead. She would have made a terrific grandma.

If Flory Sophia was alive, I could bring her to school and tell the class all about her, thought Calliope. *I bet I know a hundred things about my grandma.*

For one thing, Flory Sophia had been a great knitter. Calliope had a pair of her mittens and a lacy shawl.

Calliope took out the lacy shawl that Flory Sophia had made. She wrapped herself in the shawl. It felt just like a hug.

Calliope stared at the mirror. She felt the air whistle in the space between her two front teeth. She made the freckles on her face dance. She rubbed her hands together.

Flory Sophia was dead, but she was still Calliope's grandmother. Now and forever. One grandmother for one kid.

"Flory Sophia," Calliope whispered. "My grandmother."

one grandmother for one kid

Grandparents Day

Calliope lugged a brown grocery bag to her desk. She slipped into her seat.

"Welcome to Grandparents Day at Jackson Magnet," announced Mrs. Fennessey. "I'm so pleased to have you all with us."

Calliope looked around the room and counted twenty-five grandparents.

"I look forward to learning something about each one of our special guests. Who would like to be first?" asked Mrs. Fennessey. "Howie?"

"My grandma Gardenia Smith is the best baker in the whole wide world," said Howie. "Just wait till you taste her sweet-potato pie."

"Barf," said Stinky Stern. Mrs. Fennessey called on him next.

Stinky Stern's grandfather looked just like Santa Claus. Calliope blinked twice. *He's not his real grandfather,* she thought.

"When my grandpa Bernie Stern was in school," said Stinky, "he used to let frogs loose in class. All the kids would scream."

It's his real grandpa—no doubt about it.

Lots of kids wanted to be next. Mrs. Fennessey chose Oliver H.

Oliver H. read a poem about his special friend, Mrs. Martinez.

More kids introduced their grandparents. Some

had even brought two. Calliope tried hard to listen to them. Then Mrs. Fennessey called on Pa Lia.

"My grandmother Ka Ghee Moua was born in Laos," said Pa Lia. "She sews *paj ntaub*, 'story cloths.' She made this one for me. Grandma learned to sew from *her* grandmother. Now Grandma Ka Ghee is teaching me."

Pa Lia and her grandmother sat

down. Everyone in the class had had a turn. Everyone but Calliope. The Grandparents Day Welcome was over.

Calliope clutched her grocery bag. It felt soft and rumpled. She raised her hand.

"I want to talk about my grandma," Calliope said softly.

"We would love to hear about your grandmother, Calliope," said Mrs. Fennessey.

"Her grandma is a ghost." Stinky snickered. His grandpa laughed.

Calliope felt glued to her chair. *Maybe this was a bad idea.*

Flory Sophia

Calliope put her grocery bag on Mrs. Fennessey's desk.

"She's probably got her little old granny in there," said Stinky Stern.

Calliope gave Stinky a dirty look.

"My grandma's name was Flory Sophia Turnip-seed," Calliope began in a quiet voice. "She was tall and big, like me. She had freckles and a space between her front teeth, just like I do."

Calliope took the picture of Flory Sophia out of her bag. She showed the class. "My grand-mother was the best knitter in West Branch,

42

Iowa," said Calliope. She reached into her bag again.

"My grandma Flory Sophia made this shawl. It was knitted on the tiniest needles, size zero-zero-zero," said Calliope. She put the shawl on. She wanted everyone to see how beautiful it was. "It has over a million stitches. My grandma knitted it with such fine yarn, she could pull this entire shawl through her wedding ring."

Calliope cleared her throat. "My grandma Flory Sophia raised chickens on her farm. And she studied the stars at night. She knew the names of all the constellations. She had a hen named Little Dipper and a rooster named Orion, a cat named Cassiopeia and a dog named Taurus."

Calliope's voice quivered. She took a deep breath and silently counted to ten.

"I know a lot about my grandma," Calliope continued. "And even though she died before I was born, she is still a part of me."

Calliope's mouth was dry. She had talked for a long time, longer than anyone else. Maybe *too* long.

She grabbed her grocery bag and went back to her seat. She closed her eyes. She wished she had never come to school today. She wished she were at home in her bed, under her covers, fast asleep. Calliope opened her eyes.

Everyone was looking at her.

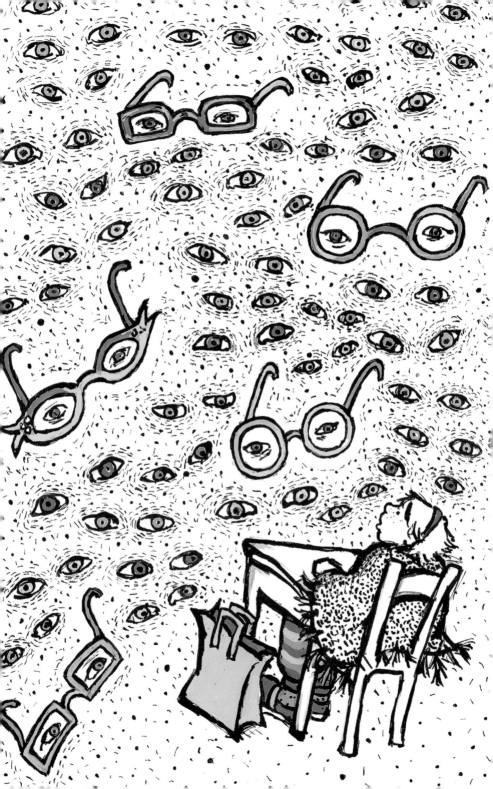

Pie

"Thank you, Calliope. Your grand-mother sounds like she was a wonderful person. I wish we could have met her," said Mrs. Fennessey. "And I want to thank all my students and their wonderful grandmothers and grandfathers and special friends. It was great learning about all of you."

Calliope covered her face with her grandma's shawl. She hoped everyone had stopped staring at her.

"Can we eat now?" asked Stinky Stern.

Calliope chewed on the soft wool of her shawl. She couldn't wait for Grandparents Day to be over.

"Yes, Matthew, it's refreshment time," announced Mrs. Fennessey.

Calliope felt a gentle hand on her shoulder. "Calliope James, that was real special," said Grandma Gardenia.

Calliope peeked out from under her shawl.

"I just know that if your grandma were alive and here today, she would be so proud of you." Grandma Gardenia gave Calliope a loud and wet kiss.

Calliope felt warm all over. *Grandma Gardenia thinks Flory Sophia would be proud of me.* She took off her shawl and put it in the grocery bag. She looked up. Pa Lia and Ka Ghee were smiling at her.

"My grandma says that you are a very good grand-daughter," said Pa Lia. Calliope grinned. *Ka Ghee thinks I am a good granddaughter!* Calliope reached into her grocery bag. Her grandma's shawl was still warm. She dug deeper. She found the picture of Flory Sophia and put it in her pocket.

Stinky Stern sneaked up behind Calliope and pulled her hair.

"Ouch!" she said.

"My, what big teeth you have, Granny."

"All the better to eat you with." Calliope growled at him.

Stinky looked surprised. His grandpa slapped her five. *Grandparents Day wasn't so bad after all.*

Calliope walked over to the refreshment table. "Grandma Gardenia," she said, "I'm ready for that pie!"

The End? Not quite!
Turn the page to find out more
about the Jackson Friends....

Pa Lia Vang

- has an older brother, Tou Ger
- loves to draw butterflies and mice
- is learning to turn cartwheels
- favorite food: noodles

Read more about Pa Lia in *Pa Lia's First Day:*

Pa Lia's first day at Jackson Magnet isn't going so well. She doesn't know anyone there. She can't find her second-grade classroom. But worst of all, she accidentally gets the only kids who have been nice to her in trouble. Will Pa Lia ever fit in?

Calliope Turnipseed James

- has one dog named Woof and zero grandparents
- loves to do math
- is learning to knit
- favorite food: Snickers

Read more about Calliope in this book, *Zero Grandparents*:

Mrs. Fennessey's class is planning a big celebration for Grandparents Day. Everyone is really excited—everyone except Calliope. Her best friends, Howie and Pa Lia, are bringing their grandmas. Even Stinky Stern's grandpa is coming. But Calliope doesn't have a grandma *or* a grandpa. How can she celebrate without a grandparent of her very own?

Howardina Geraldina Paulina Maxina Gardenia Smith

★ has a brand-new red ten-speed bike
★ loves to sing
★ is learning to use all the gears on her brand-new red ten-speed bike
★ favorite food: Grandma Gardenia's cookies

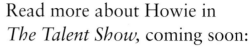

Read more about Howie in *The Talent Show,* coming soon:

Jackson Magnet is having a talent show. Howie, Pa Lia, Calliope, and Stinky Stern are all in it. Howie is scared. Everyone—mothers, fathers, grandparents, neighbors, teachers, kids, even the Channel Seven News—will be there watching her sing. Will Howie make it through her big night?

Matthew "Stinky" Stern

- has a pet parakeet named Petey
- loves being a stinker
- is learning to ride a two-wheeler, with no hands
- favorite food: cowboy baked beans

Read more about Stinky in…

Hang on a minute. Does Stinky deserve a book? You'll have to wait and see!

DATE DUE

DEMCO 38-296